ALFIE

Alfie's Feet

Shirley Hughes

Red Fox

This little pig went to market,

This little pig stayed at home,

This little pig had roast beef,

This little pig had none,

And this little pig cried, Wee-wee-wee-wee-wee,

I can't find my way home.

ALFIE

Puddles and Parties

Shirley Hughes

Red Fox

Alfie's Feet: For Edward and Catherine
Alfie Gives a Hand: For Jamie and Henry

Other titles in the Alfie series:

Alfie Gets in First
An Evening at Alfie's
Alfie and the Birthday Surprise
Alfie Wins a Prize
Alfie and the Big Boys
Alfie Weather
Alfie's World
Annie Rose is my Little Sister
Rhymes for Annie Rose
The Big Alfie and Annie Rose Storybook
The Big Alfie Out of Doors Storybook

ALFIE: PUDDLES AND PARTIES
A RED FOX BOOK 978 1 849 41472 2

This edition published 2011, exclusively for Sainsbury's by Red Fox,
an imprint of Random House Children's Books
A Random House Group Company

1 3 5 7 9 10 8 6 4 2

Copyright © Shirley Hughes, 1982, 1983, 2011

ALFIE'S FEET
First published in Great Britain by The Bodley Head in 1982
Red Fox edition first published in 1993

ALFIE GIVES A HAND
First published in Great Britain by The Bodley Head in 1983
Red Fox edition first published in 1994

The right of Shirley Hughes to be identified as the author and illustrator of this work has been asserted in accordance
with the Copyright, Designs and Patents Act 1988.

Red Fox Books are published by Random House Children's Books, 61–63 Uxbridge Road, London W5 5SA

www.kidsatrandomhouse.co.uk
www.rbooks.co.uk

Addresses for companies within The Random House Group Limited can be found at: www.randomhouse.co.uk/offices.htm

THE RANDOM HOUSE GROUP Limited Reg. No. 954009

A CIP catalogue record for this book is available from the British Library.

Printed in China

Alfie had a little sister called Annie Rose.
Alfie's feet were quite big. Annie Rose's feet
were rather small. They were all soft and pink
underneath. Alfie knew a game he could play
with Annie Rose, counting her toes.

Annie Rose had lots of different ways of getting about. She went forwards, crawling,

and backwards, on her behind,

and she liked to slide about very fast on her potty,

skidding round and round
on the floor and in and out
of the table legs.

Annie Rose had
some new red shoes.

She could walk in them
a bit, if she was pushing her
little cart or holding on to
someone's hand.

When they went out, Annie Rose wore her
red shoes and Alfie wore his old brown ones.
Mum usually helped him put them on, because
he wasn't very good at doing up the laces yet.

If it had been raining Alfie
liked to go stamping about in
mud and walking through puddles,

splish, splash, SPLOSH!

Then his shoes got rather wet.

So did his socks,

and so did his feet.

So one Saturday morning Alfie and Mum went to
a big shop in the High Street.

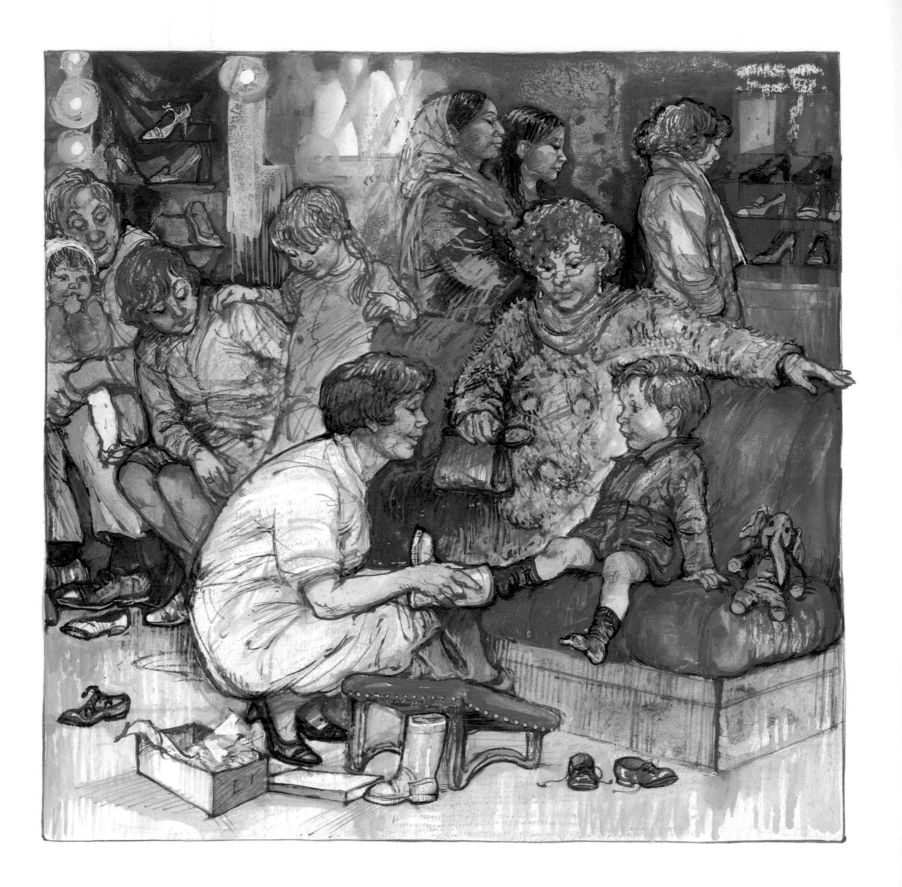

They bought a pair of shiny new yellow boots for Alfie to wear when he went stamping about in mud and walking through puddles. Alfie was very pleased. He carried them home himself in a cardboard box.

When they got in, Alfie sat down at once and unwrapped his new boots. He put them on all by himself and walked about in them,

stamp! stamp! stamp!

He went into the kitchen to show Mum and Dad and Annie Rose, stamping his feet all the way,

stamp! stamp! stamp!

The boots were very smart
and shiny but they felt funny.

Alfie wanted to go out again right away. So he put on his mac, and Dad took his book and his newspaper and they went off to the park.

Alfie stamped in a lot of mud and walked through a
lot of puddles, splish, splash, SPLOSH! He frightened
some sparrows who were having a bath. He even
frightened two big ducks. They went hurrying back
to their pond, walking with their feet turned in.

Alfie looked down at his feet. They still
felt funny. They kept turning outwards.
Dad was sitting on a bench. They both
looked at Alfie's feet.

Suddenly Alfie knew what was wrong!

Dad lifted Alfie on to the bench beside him and helped him to take off each boot and put it on the other foot. And when Alfie stood down again his feet didn't feel a bit funny any more.

After tea Mum painted a big black R on to one of Alfie's boots and a big black L on the other to help Alfie remember which boot was which. The R was for Right foot and the L was for Left foot. The black paint wore off in the end and the boots stopped being new and shiny, but Alfie usually did remember to get them on the proper way round after that. They felt much better when he went stamping about in mud and walking through puddles.

And, of course, Annie Rose made such a fuss about Alfie having new boots that she had to have a pair of her own to go stamping about in too, splish, splash, SPLOSH!

ALFIE

Alfie Gives a Hand

Shirley Hughes

Red Fox

One day Alfie came home from Nursery
School with a card in an envelope. His best
friend, Bernard, had given it to him.

"Look, it's got my name on it," said
Alfie, pointing.

Mum said that it was an invitation to
Bernard's birthday tea party.

"Will it be at Bernard's house?" Alfie wanted to know. He'd never been there before. Mum said yes, and she told him all about birthday parties, and how you had to take a present, and about the games and how there would be nice things to eat.

Alfie was very excited about Bernard's party. When the day came Mum washed Alfie's face and brushed his hair and helped him put on a clean T-shirt and his brand-new shorts.

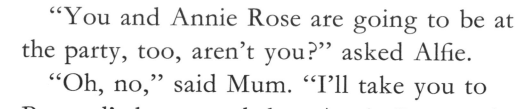

"You and Annie Rose are going to be at the party, too, aren't you?" asked Alfie.

"Oh, no," said Mum. "I'll take you to Bernard's house and then Annie Rose and I will go to the park and come back to collect you when it's time to go home."

"But I want you to be there," said Alfie.

Mum told him that she and Annie Rose hadn't been invited to the party, only Alfie, because he was Bernard's special friend.

"You don't mind my leaving you at Nursery School, do you?" she said. "So you won't mind being at Bernard's house either, as soon as you get there."

Mum had bought some crayons for Alfie to give Bernard for his birthday present. While she was wrapping them up, Alfie went upstairs. He looked under his pillow and found his old bit of blanket which he kept in bed with him at night.

He brought it downstairs, and sat down to wait for Mum.

"You won't want your old blanket
at the party," said Mum, when
it was time to go.

But Alfie wouldn't leave
his blanket behind. He held
it tightly with one hand,
and Bernard's present with
the other, all the way to
Bernard's house.

When they got there, Bernard's Mum opened the door.
"Hello, Alfie," she said. "Let's go into the garden
and find Bernard and the others."
Then Mum gave Alfie a kiss and said good-bye,
and went off to the park with Annie Rose.

"Would you like to put your blanket down here with the coats?" asked Bernard's Mum. But Alfie didn't want to put his blanket down. He still held on to it very tightly.

Bernard was in the garden with Min and Sam and Daniel and some other children from the Nursery School.

"Happy birthday!" Alfie
remembered to say, and he
gave Bernard his present.
Bernard pulled off the paper.

"Crayons! How lovely!"
said Bernard's Mum. "Say
thank you, Bernard."
"Thank you," said
Bernard. But do you
know what he did then?

He threw the crayons up in the air. They landed all over the grass.

"That was a silly thing to do," said Bernard's Mum, as she picked up the crayons and put them away.

Then Bernard's Mum brought out some bubble stuff
and blew lots of bubbles into the air. They floated all
over the garden and the children jumped about trying
to pop them.

Alfie couldn't pop many bubbles because he was holding
on to his blanket. But Bernard jumped about and pushed
and popped more bubbles than anyone else.

"Don't push people, Bernard," said Bernard's Mum sternly.

One huge bubble landed lightly on Min's sleeve. It stayed there, quivering and shiny. Min smiled. She stood very still.

Then Bernard came up
behind her and popped
the big bubble.

Min began to cry.
Bernard's Mum was
cross with Bernard and
told him to say he
was sorry.

"Never mind, we're going to have tea now, dear," she told
Min. "Who would you like to sit next to?"

Min wanted to sit next to Alfie. She stopped crying and
pulled her chair right up close to his.

For tea there were sandwiches and little sausages on sticks and crisps and jellies and a big iced cake with candles and "Happy Birthday, Bernard" written on it.

Bernard took a huge breath and blew out
all the candles at once – *Phoooooo!* Everyone
clapped and sang "Happy Birthday to You".

Then Bernard blew into his lemonade through his straw and made rude bubbling noises. He blew into his jelly, too, until his Mum took it away from him.

Alfie liked the tea . . . but holding on to his blanket made eating rather difficult. It got all mixed up with the jelly and crisps, and covered in sticky crumbs.

After tea, Bernard's Mum said that they were all going to play a game. But Bernard ran off and fetched his very best present. It was a tiger mask.

Bernard went behind a bush and came out wearing the mask and making terrible growling noises: "Grrr! Grrr, grrrr, GRRRR! ACHT!"

He went crawling round the garden,
sounding very fierce and frightening.
Min began to cry again. She clung on to
Alfie.

"Get up *at once*, Bernard," said Bernard's Mum. "It's not that kind of game. Now let's all stand in a circle, everyone, and join hands."

Bernard stopped growling, but he wouldn't take off his tiger mask. Instead he grabbed Alfie's hand to pull him into the circle.

Bernard's Mum tried to take Min's hand and bring her into the circle, too. But Min wouldn't hold anyone's hand but Alfie's. She went on crying. She cried and cried.

Then Alfie made a brave decision. He ran and put down his blanket, very carefully, in a safe place underneath the table.

Now he could hold Min's hand, too, as well as Bernard's.

Min stopped crying. She wasn't
frightened of Bernard in his tiger mask
now she was holding Alfie's hand.

She joined in the game and they all
danced round together, singing:

"Ring-a-ring-o'-roses
A pocket full of posies
A-tishoo, a-tishoo,
We all fall DOWN!"

Afterwards Alfie and Min joined in with some more games and ate ice-cream and pop-corn and bounced balloons with the others. Alfie had such a good time that his blanket stayed under the table until Mum and Annie Rose came to collect him.

"What a helpful guest you've been, Alfie," said Bernard's Mum, when Alfie thanked her and said good-bye. "Min wouldn't have enjoyed the party a bit without you. I *do* wish Bernard would learn to be helpful sometimes –

– Perhaps he will, one day."

On the way home, Alfie carried his
blanket in one hand and a balloon and a
packet of sweets in the other. His blanket
had got a bit messy at the party. It had been
rather in the way, too. Next time he thought
he might leave it safely at home, after all.